Disney
CLUB PENGUIN™

A Search-and-Find Book

D1300786

Illustrated by Richard Carbajal

Grosset & Dunlap
An Imprint of Penguin Group (USA) Inc.

ISBN 978-0-448-45390-3   10 9 8 7 6 5 4 3 2 1

Greetings, Club Penguin Fans!

Are you ready for some serious search-and-find fun?

Club Penguin is always a popular place to be, but in this book, it's jam-packed! The scenes on these pages are filled to the brim with penguins, puffles, pins, and plenty more.

Throughout the book, you'll be given special items to seek out. When you are done you can flip to the back for checklists of even *more* hidden treasures.

Ready, set . . . search!

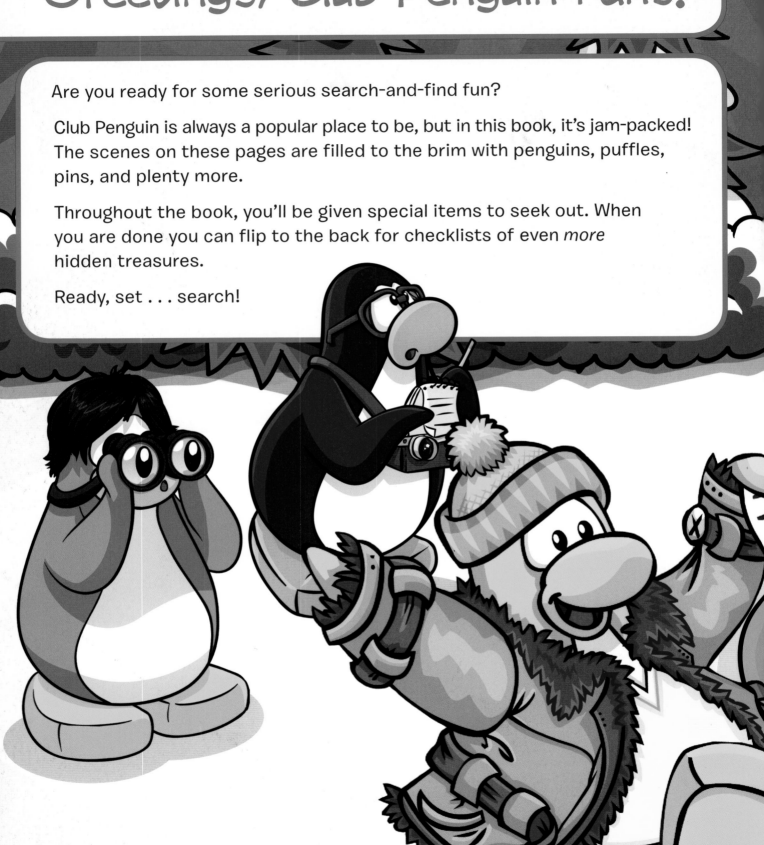

SNOWBALL FIGHT!

There's a party out in full force at the Snow Forts! Penguins from all over are wearing their favorite party costumes.

Can you find the penguin wearing swirly glasses from an April Fool's Day party?

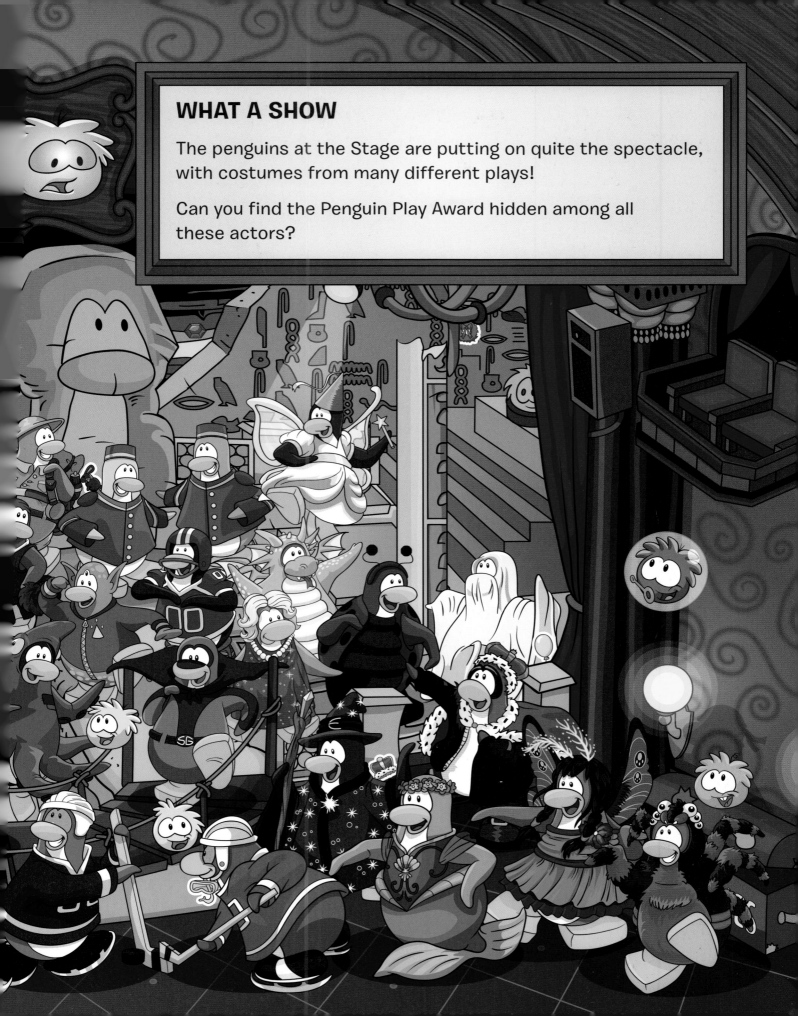

WHAT A SHOW

The penguins at the Stage are putting on quite the spectacle, with costumes from many different plays!

Can you find the Penguin Play Award hidden among all these actors?

PENGUINS AT WORK

Who says work can't be fun? These penguins at the Town Center sure know how to have a good time on the job.

Can you find 12 workers wearing hard hats?

BUST A MOVE

The Night Club is hopping, as always! Cadence leads the show while laying down some epic dance tunes.

Can you find 4 partying penguins dancing in sync?

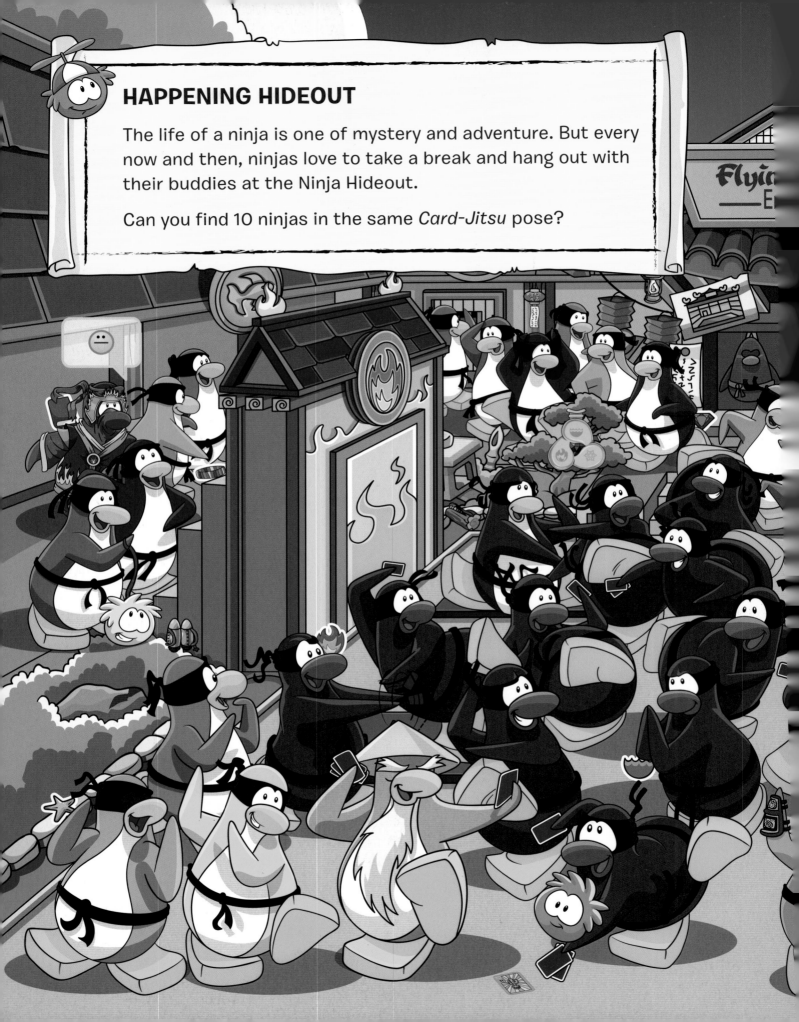

HAPPENING HIDEOUT

The life of a ninja is one of mystery and adventure. But every now and then, ninjas love to take a break and hang out with their buddies at the Ninja Hideout.

Can you find 10 ninjas in the same *Card-Jitsu* pose?

MAKING A SPLASH

Splish-splash! These penguins are having a blast at the Cove with some wet 'n' wild water sports.

Can you find the lifeguard in all this mayhem?

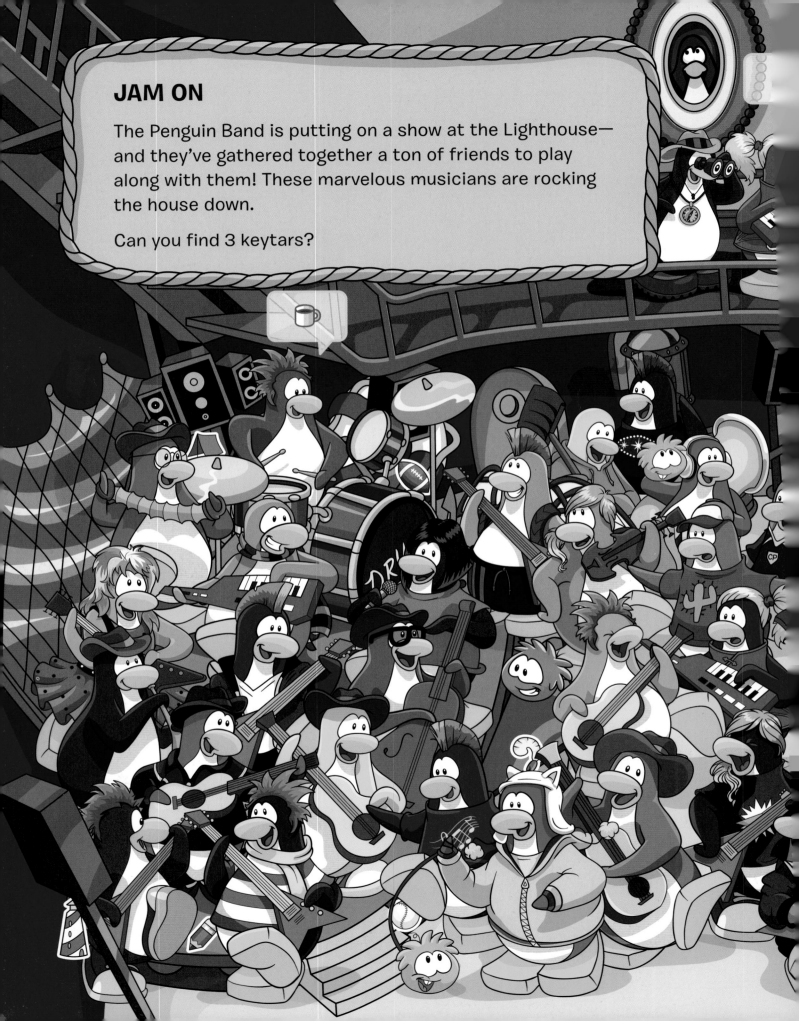

JAM ON

The Penguin Band is putting on a show at the Lighthouse—and they've gathered together a ton of friends to play along with them! These marvelous musicians are rocking the house down.

Can you find 3 keytars?

FUZZY FURBALLS

The Pet Shop is filled with furry puffles. And they're just waiting to be adopted by a fun-loving penguin like you.

Can you find the Pet Shop owner?

Each scene has lots of hidden items to seek out. Can you find them all?

SNOWBALL FIGHT!

- Aunt Arctic
- medieval knight costume
- red cheerleader
- Fall Fair ringmaster
- 3 penguins dressed as medieval princesses
- penguin dressed for Pirate Party
- 5 anniversary hats
- Beta Party Hat

WHAT A SHOW

- golden puffle
- Ruby
- Ruby's ruby
- yellow puffle
- Gamma Gal
- Shadow Guy
- 4 bellhops
- Boris the mummy
- Zip the alien

AHOY, PIRATES!

- Captain Rockhopper
- key to the Captain's Quarters
- The Journal of Captain Rockhopper
- 15 pirates wearing striped shirts
- 8 adventure scavenger hunt items
- Yarr
- a barrel
- 10 coins

PENGUINS AT WORK

- Gary
- 2 baristas
- 3 pizza chefs
- firefighter
- lifeguard
- goldsmith
- 3 Rescue Squad members
- 3 tour guides
- 5 coffee mugs

BUST A MOVE

- ☐ Cadence
- ☐ 14 records
- ☐ 7 purple puffles
- ☐ diva penguin
- ☐ break-dancing penguin
- ☐ penguin dancing in skates
- ☐ green puffle
- ☐ penguin in a tuxedo

HAPPENING HIDEOUT

- ☐ Sensei
- ☐ amulet
- ☐ 3 fire ninjas
- ☐ 8 sensei scavenger hunt items
- ☐ fire icon
- ☐ snow icon
- ☐ water icon

MAKING A SPLASH

- ☐ 6 flame surfboards
- ☐ jet pack
- ☐ scuba penguin
- ☐ silver surfboard
- ☐ orange puffle
- ☐ life ring
- ☐ 9 penguins wearing flowery shorts
- ☐ penguin wearing a Hawaiian lei

JAM ON

- ☐ Penguin Band
- ☐ 3 tubas
- ☐ violin
- ☐ 18 guitars (regular and double)
- ☐ Find all 6 Music Jam shirts
- ☐ 2 trombones
- ☐ 2 basses

FUZZY FURBALLS

- ☐ 14 blue puffles
- ☐ 15 purple puffles
- ☐ 10 black puffles
- ☐ 20 red puffles
- ☐ 11 orange puffles
- ☐ 17 yellow puffles
- ☐ 17 green puffles
- ☐ 23 white puffles
- ☐ 16 pink puffles

Look for these items throughout the book:

- ☐ 8 buoys
- ☐ blue Viking Helmet
- ☐ can of worms

- ☐ 4 secret agents
- ☐ 22 ninja shadows
- ☐ red Viking Helmet

- ☐ Herbert P. Bear
- ☐ Klutzy the Crab
- ☐ Herbert's footprints

PINS

SNOWBALL FIGHT!

PENGUINS AT WORK

MAKING A SPLASH

WHAT A SHOW

BUST A MOVE

JAM ON

AHOY, PIRATES!

HAPPENING HIDEOUT

FUZZY FURBALLS